Dear Parent:

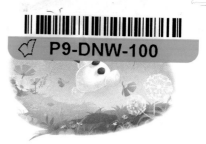

Congratulations! Your child is taking the first steps on an exciting journey. The destination? Independent reading!

STEP INTO READING® will help your child get there. The program offers five steps to reading success. Each step includes fun stories and colorful art. There are also Step into Reading Sticker Books, Step into Reading Math Readers, Step into Reading Phonics Readers, Step into Reading Write-In Readers, and Step into Reading Phonics Boxed Sets—a complete literacy program with something for every child.

Learning to Read, Step by Step!

Ready to Read   Preschool–Kindergarten
• big type and easy words • rhyme and rhythm • picture clues
For children who know the alphabet and are eager to begin reading.

Reading with Help   Preschool–Grade 1
• basic vocabulary • short sentences • simple stories
For children who recognize familiar words and sound out new words with help.

Reading on Your Own   Grades 1–3
• engaging characters • easy-to-follow plots • popular topics
For children who are ready to read on their own.

Reading Paragraphs   Grades 2–3
• challenging vocabulary • short paragraphs • exciting stories
For newly independent readers who read simple sentences with confidence.

Ready for Chapters   Grades 2–4
• chapters • longer paragraphs • full-color art
For children who want to take the plunge into chapter books but still like colorful pictures.

STEP INTO READING® is designed to give every child a successful reading experience. The grade levels are only guides. Children can progress through the steps at their own speed, developing confidence in their reading, no matter what their grade.

Remember, a lifetime love of reading starts with a single step!

FROZEN
STORY COLLECTION

Step into Reading, Random House, and the Random House colophon are registered trademarks
of Random House LLC.

Visit us on the Web!
StepIntoReading.com
randomhousekids.com

Educators and librarians, for a variety of teaching tools, visit us at
RHTeachersLibrarians.com

ISBN 978-0-7364-3435-5

MANUFACTURED IN THE UNITED STATES
10 9 8 7 6 5 4 3 2

STEP INTO READING®

Disney FROZEN

FROZEN
STORY COLLECTION

Step 1 and 2 Books

A Collection of Five Early Readers

Random House 🏠 New York

CONTENTS

ELSA

- Queen of Arendelle
- Best friend and sister to Anna
- Has the power to control ice and snow
- Quote: "LET IT GO!"

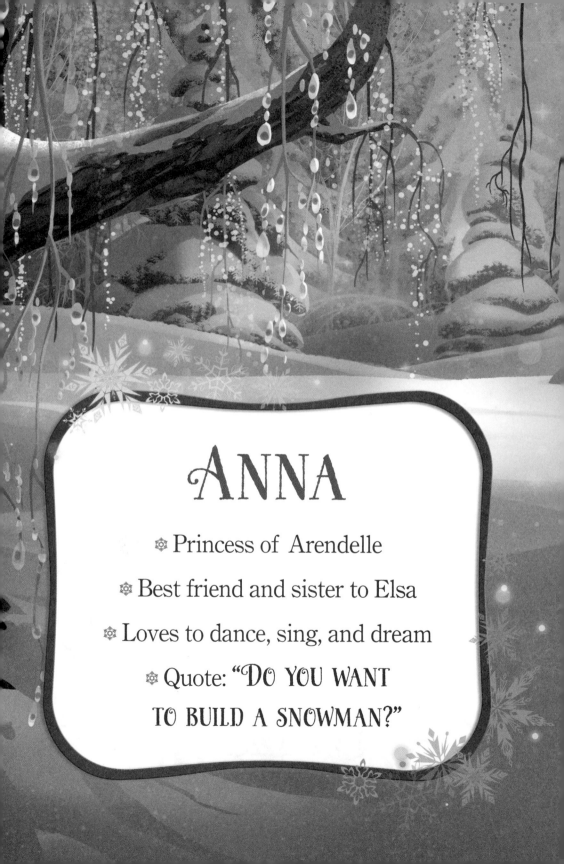

ANNA

❄ Princess of Arendelle

❄ Best friend and sister to Elsa

❄ Loves to dance, sing, and dream

❄ Quote: "DO YOU WANT
TO BUILD A SNOWMAN?"

OLAF

❄ Magical snowman made by Elsa

❄ Enjoys making new friends

❄ Loves spending time in the sun

❄ Quote: "I'M OLAF, AND
I LIKE WARM HUGS!"

KRISTOFF

- Harvests ice from the mountain lakes
- Best friend is his reindeer, Sven
- Grew up with magical trolls
- Quote: "ICE IS MY LIFE!"

Sven

- Loyal reindeer to best friend, Kristoff
- Pulls wooden sled full of supplies
- Loves to eat carrots
- Enjoys icy adventures

MARSHMALLOW

- ❄ Huge magical snowman
- ❄ Protects Queen Elsa's ice palace
- ❄ Scares off unwelcome guests
- ❄ Quote: "GO AWAY!"

HANS

* Prince of the Southern Isles

* Youngest of 13 brothers

* Biggest goal is to be king

* Quote: "I LOVE CRAZY!"

TROLLS

❄ Live in a valley near Arendelle

❄ Raised Kristoff and Sven

❄ Able to change into rocks at will

❄ Quote: "KRISTOFF'S HOME!"

STEP INTO READING®

1

STEP

READY TO READ

DISNEY
FROZEN

BIG SNOWMAN, LITTLE SNOWMAN

By Tish Rabe

Illustrated by the Disney Storybook Art Team

Random House 🏠 New York

HAPPY sister.

SAD sister.

At first,
Hans seems nice.

Elsa runs away.
She makes the
snow and ice!

Anna gets ON her horse.
Ride, Anna, ride!

Anna falls OFF.

It's cold outside.

Anna meets Kristoff.

His reindeer is Sven.

Kristoff goes IN . . .

then OUT again!

Anna and Kristoff
go, go, go!
Sven climbs FAST.

Anna climbs SLOW.

Elsa has a palace.

Anna enters FIRST.

Kristoff enters LAST.

Elsa freezes Anna
with an icy blast!

COLD Olaf dreams
of the HOT, HOT sun.

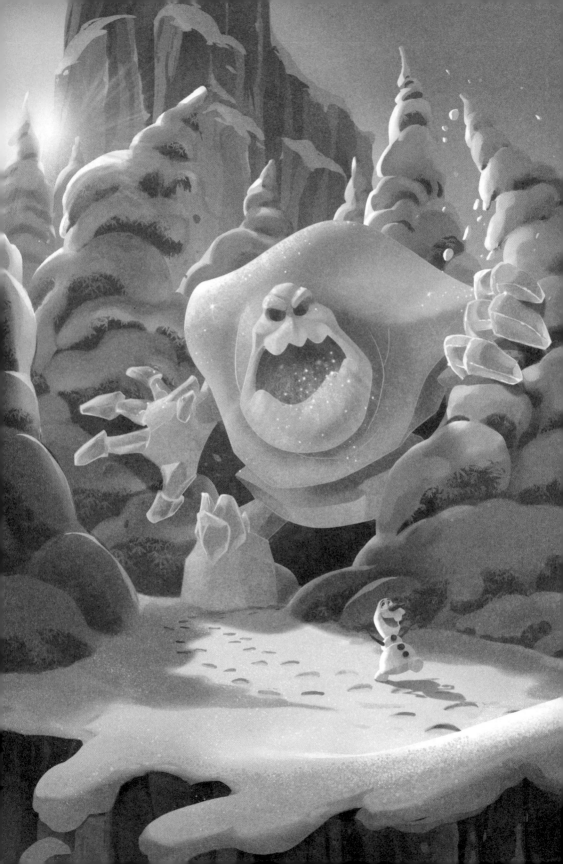

LITTLE snowman.

BIG snowman!

Run! Run! Run!

Anna is freezing.

She is worried, too.

She asks a troll
what to do.

Watch out!
Hans attacks!

Anna is in FRONT.
Elsa is in BACK.

Winter ENDS.

Summer STARTS.

Anna's act of love
has thawed
her frozen heart.

Olaf APART.

Sisters TOGETHER.

Elsa, Anna, and Olaf . . .

friends forever!

HELLO, OLAF!

By Andrea Posner-Sanchez

Random House 🏠 New York

This is Olaf.

He is a snowman.

Elsa made a snowman
to play with when she
was a little girl.
Elsa and Anna called
the snowman Olaf.
They pretended he
was alive.

Years later, Elsa uses
her magical powers
to really make Olaf
come to life!

Anna is all
grown up now.
Olaf meets Anna,
Kristoff, and Sven.

Sven loves carrots.

Olaf better hold on
to his nose!

Olaf wishes for
warm days and
sunshine.

A day on the beach
would be a dream
come true!

Olaf would sail.

Olaf would swim.

He would even sit
in a hot tub.
Do not melt, Olaf!

Elsa has a way
to keep Olaf cold
even when it is warm.

She does some magic.

Now Olaf the snowman
will never melt!

Disney
FROZEN

A Tale of Two Sisters

By Melissa Lagonegro

Illustrated by Maria Elena Naggi, Studio IBOIX,
and the Disney Storybook Art Team

Random House 🏠 New York

Princess Elsa
and Princess Anna
are sisters.

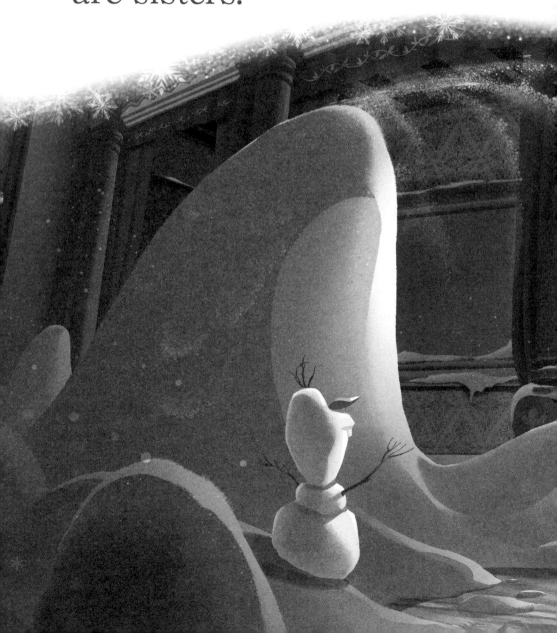

Elsa has a secret.

She has magic powers.

She can create ice.

Elsa makes a mistake.

Her magic hits Anna.

Anna is very cold.

Their parents worry.

Anna gets warm again.
She wants to be friends
with her big sister.

To keep Anna safe,

Elsa stays away.

It makes Elsa sad.

Anna and Elsa grow up.
Anna meets Prince Hans.
They fall in love.

Elsa becomes queen.

The kingdom cheers.

Anna wants
to marry Hans.
Elsa says no.
Anna and Elsa argue.
Anna pulls off
Elsa's glove.

Magic ice shoots
from Elsa's hand.

Elsa runs far away.
She does not want
her magic
to hurt anyone.

Elsa covers the land
with snow.
She makes an ice palace.

The kingdom needs Elsa
to stop the storm.
There is so much snow!
Anna must find Elsa.

Anna meets Kristoff
and his reindeer, Sven.
They help her search
for Elsa.

They meet Olaf.

He is a nice snowman.

He leads them to Elsa.

The kingdom worries
about Anna.
Hans will find her.

Anna finally finds Elsa.
She tells Elsa
to come home.

Elsa is afraid
she might hurt someone.
Anna will not listen.

Elsa grows angry.
She blasts Anna
with a bolt of ice.

Elsa makes
a giant snowman.
He chases
Anna and her friends
out of the palace.

Elsa's blast is turning
Anna to ice!
An old troll helps Anna.

He says an act
of true love
can save her.

Hans finds Elsa.
His guards
bring her home.

Hans will not kiss Anna.

He does not love her.

He just wants
to rule the kingdom.

Anna is almost frozen.

Kristoff loves Anna.

His kiss might save her.

But Elsa needs Anna's help!

Hans tries to hurt Elsa.
Anna blocks his sword
when she freezes solid.

Elsa is safe.

She cries.

She hugs Anna.

Anna starts to melt!

Her act of love

has saved their lives.

The sisters
are best friends
at last!

DISNEY
FROZEN

ANNA'S BEST FRIENDS

By Christy Webster

Illustrated by the Disney Storybook Art Team

Random House New York

Olaf the snowman
is Anna's friend.

He dreams
of warmer weather.

Reindeer Sven is
Kristoff's friend.

They always
stick together.

A frozen adventure
in a sleigh.

Run, Sven, run!

Get away!

Anna explores

the ice and snow.

Her friends tell her
which way to go.

Anna's sister, Elsa,
makes magical ice.

Sometimes sisters disagree.

Sometimes they are nice.

Sven is brave.

He pulls the sled

higher.

Olaf is brave.

He builds Anna a fire.

Now Anna's adventures
are done.

She and her friends have
some fun!

Elsa, Kristoff,
Olaf, and Sven.

They will always be Anna's best friends!

Disney

FROZEN

THE CHRISTMAS PARTY

By Andrea Posner-Sanchez

Illustrated by the Disney Storybook Art Team

Random House 🏠 New York

It is almost Christmas!
Elsa invites
the whole kingdom
to celebrate.

Elsa uses her magic
to make ice sculptures.
Anna brings out
treats.

Sven helps
decorate the tree.

Kristoff practices
singing carols.

Olaf bakes
Christmas cookies.

Elsa makes sure
he does not get
too close to the oven!

The closets are
stuffed with gifts.

The desserts are ready.

Everything inside
the castle looks great.
Anna wants Elsa
to look outside.

The sisters go
to the window.

The villagers are
having fun.

They love
the snow and ice!

"We have worked hard,"
Anna tells Elsa.
"We can have some fun!"

The sisters go outside
to play in the snow.

They have a
snowball fight!

"This is fun!"
says Elsa.
But soon it is time
to get ready
for the party.

Later, Anna knocks
on Elsa's door.
Elsa opens it
and smiles.

Parties are great,
but sisters are the best!